# Charmed

Carrie Mac

orca soundings

ORCA BOOK PUBLISHERS

**Library and Archives Canada Cataloguing in Publication**

Mac, Carrie, 1975-
Charmed / Carrie Mac.

(Orca soundings)
ISBN 10: 1-55143-321-4
ISBN 13: 978-1-55143-321-9
I. Title. II. Series.

PS8625.A23C43 2004 jC813'.6 C2004-904721-3

First published in the United States, 2004
**Library of Congress Control Number:** 2004110934

**Summary:** Izzy finds she is one in a long line of girls ensnared in prostitution, with no way to escape.

Orca Book Publishers gratefully acknowledges the support for its publishing programs provided by the following agencies: the Government of Canada through the Book Publishing Industry Development Program and the Canada Council for the Arts, and the Province of British Columbia through the BC Arts Council and the Book Publishing Tax Credit.

Cover design by Lynn O'Rourke
Cover photography by Eyewire

Orca Book Publishers
PO Box 5626, Stn. B
Victoria, BC Canada
V8R 6S4

Orca Book Publishers
PO Box 468
Custer, WA USA
98240-0468

www.orcabook.com
Printed and bound in Canada.
Printed on 100% PCW recycled paper.

13 12 11 10 • 7 6 5 4

*For Renée—*
*brave, strong and smart.*

# Chapter One

We're at a Chinese restaurant, the Golden City, or the Cold and Gritty, as Rob calls it. He pulls back the corners of his eyes and orders in a bad Chinese accent. My mother laughs nervously, tossing me a please-don't-start-anything look when Rob isn't watching. I'd like to tip his tea into his lap and apologize to the crowded room for him being such a racist prick, but it's the night before Mom goes up north to cook in the logging camp, and I don't want to ruin it for her.

Margaret cringes and stares at her plate, even though there's nothing on it yet. The last time she came out with us for supper was for Mom's birthday. We went to a really expensive French restaurant. The food was amazing. Just as Rob was finishing his chocolate mousse, he bellowed, "Waiter! Waiter! There's a cockroach on my plate!" He'd actually brought one with him! From home! He argued with the manager for almost half an hour before the manager finally agreed to give us the entire meal for free.

Margaret slept over that night. She told me she was very sorry, and yes, she was and would always be my best friend, but she just couldn't bear going out to dinner with us ever again, not so long as Mom was dating Rob the Slob.

"He lied! It was so embarrassing. He is so gross, Izzy," she said in the middle of the night as she stuffed a wad of marshmallows into her mouth. Talk about gross.

"He's not so bad." Honestly, I hate the ground he walks on, I hate the air he breathes, I wish him dead on a regular basis, but all the same, I was pissed off that Margaret was acting all high-and-mighty about it.

She only agreed to come this time because Mom begged her, and as much as Margaret can't stand Rob, she adores my mother.

Rob is so bad with chopsticks you have to watch, like how you just can't look away from a car crash. I don't know why the idiot doesn't use a fork. Margaret isn't saying much; she never does around Rob because he calls her Margarine. I told him not to. I told him she's sensitive about being fat. He says it has nothing to do with how fat she is; it just rhymes with her name. I was going to tell the genius that margarine doesn't actually rhyme with Margaret, but my mother gave me another one of those looks, so I kept my trap shut.

Just when I'm thinking the night cannot get worse, it does. Cody Dillon, man of my dreams, walks into the restaurant with two gorgeous girls I think I recognize from school. I slide down in my seat and hiss at Margaret to do the same. They walk by.

"Lose something, Margarine?" Rob says as we sit back up. Margaret pushes her plate away, her cheeks flushed.

"Shut up, Rob!" I throw a fortune cookie at him. He catches it, cracks it open and pretends to read the fortune.

"Ancient Chinese proverb say bad rittle girls get in big trouble." Rob sits back, folds his arms and nods at my mother. "You gonna let her talk to me like that?"

"Margaret doesn't like it when you call her that, Rob. He's sorry, Margaret, okay?"

Margaret barely nods her head. Mom winks at her.

"And as for you, Izzy, you and Rob are going to have to figure out a way of being nice to each other while I'm gone. Six months is a long time. You'd both be doing yourselves a favor if you started off on the right foot."

Six months stuck with Rob the Slob. I'd rethink my alternatives, but there are none.

"How about you two walk home?" Mom says. "It's a nice night out."

"Yeah, Margarine could use the walk," Rob adds, and laughs when I fake a lunge at him.

Margaret can't get out of there fast enough. I take my time. Maybe Cody

Dillon will look up and notice me, but why would he when he's got two supermodels glued to him?

"Did you see Cody Dillon come in?" I ask Margaret once we're outside.

"Who?"

Margaret is a little slow sometimes.

"Cody Dillon! He dropped out last year?"

"And that makes him cool?"

No, his wolf blue eyes, his Jeep cruising past with the bass thumping, his worn jeans and tight T-shirts, his muscled arms and the way he can just glance in your direction and make you feel as if you're all of a sudden the center of the universe. All that makes him cool, but that sort of thing is lost on Margaret. Mom says she's a late bloomer. I love Margaret, I really do, but sometimes I wonder if she'll ever bloom at all.

# Chapter Two

I finally have my Very Own Cody Dillon Moment today. I'm just coming out of the corner store on the way to school, and he's just going in, but the door kind of jams, and he kind of bumps me, and I drop my math text and my lunch bag and the pack of gum I just bought. He picks it all up and hands it back to me all slow, eyes on mine.

"Sorry," he says, and then the two girls he's with, the ones from the Chinese restaurant, are all, "Um, Cody? Hello?" He puts up his hand. They shut up and roll their eyes, hands on their hips, belly buttons exposed even though that's against school rules. One of them has a pierced belly button. It's not like I'm some kind of prude or anything; I actually like the way it looks, but it's just that belly button piercings are even more against the rules, so, um, hello? How To Get Kicked Out Of School In One Easy Lesson—get your belly button pierced and show it off. Duh.

He takes my hand (TAKES MY HAND!) and kisses the back of it (KISSES THE BACK OF IT!) and says, "My apologies" in an English accent, even though he's from Vancouver.

When I tell Margaret, she's all, "So what, Izzy? So your planets crashed for a second. Let me remind you, Cody Dillon is not from our planet. He's a dropout."

I don't talk to her for the rest of the class. By the time the bell rings, she's apologizing to me.

"Sorry. He's not that bad," she says. "I guess."

"You guess he's not that bad?" This is an apology?

"Well, he is kind of a badass."

"With a nice ass." I decide to let it go at that. Margaret has no idea what she's talking about when it comes to boys. Men. The badasses are the best ones. The boring ones are just that: BORING.

But then there are the Robs of the world. Mom picks those. They seem like cool badasses at first, but then they turn out to be lazy slobs. Rob the Slob is the king of that particular population.

## Chapter Three

Reliving my Cody Dillon Moment takes up most of my time. I don't have much time left over to care that Rob the Slob hasn't said one word to me since Mom left. I did a test. I made him macaroni and cheese seven nights in a row and he still didn't say a word, even though there was meat in the fridge going bad.

When Mom gets back, he'll rat on me and she'll do all the freaking out he's too lazy to do. On the eighth night I add hot dogs (not moldy or stinky, probably still good) and some real cheese (slices), and make toast too, just so he can't say I didn't try. I just know it: she'll come back and he'll sit her on the couch, and then he'll bring out the list of all the things I did wrong while she was gone and pace in front of her, reading right from the list.

My crimes? Let the laundry pile up, didn't do the dishes, forgot to let his dumb dog out so it pissed on the floor, and of course that's my fault too, nicked his cigarettes, skipped school and got caught. There's more, I bet. I bet he's waiting for Mom to come home so he can lay out how I ruin his life and it would be much better if I went and lived with my dad. Yeah, right. I'd rather fall off a cliff and break my neck. Like living with a manic-depressive freak who never leaves his spider-infested basement suite would be anything other than unbearable. That man collects dead spiders. He fills up entire jars with them. Mom says he wasn't always like that, but how would I know? When I was two, just before he went to the loony bin the first time, he burnt down our house. There are no photos or anything else from the so-called good times to prove that he wasn't always a psycho freak. Live with my dad? I think not. Not in a million years.

Hey, maybe my dad and Rob could be roommates. Rob will need someplace else to live soon enough because I'm keeping my own list. We'll see who Mom picks. How about this? Rob NEVER does anything around the house, even though he swore he'd fix the bathroom taps, paint the hallway and replace the rotting floorboards in the kitchen while she was in camp. He doesn't even take his crusty laundry out of the bathroom. And he has poker nights here, even though Mom said she didn't want any gambling in this house. Plus he knocked over her expensive perfume and spilled it all, and now the house stinks of it and she's going to flip. And I never get to watch TV because he hogs it all the time. All he ever watches is the sports channel, which is funny because he never gets off his ass to do anything, let alone play sports. Want to know what tops the list? My ace in the hole? When he does actually get his slobby self out of the house, sometimes he doesn't come home at night at all. What am I supposed to think about that, huh?

We'll see who Mom picks: some greasy unemployed mill worker she'd only been dating for seven months before she went up north, or her very own flesh and blood, me, her daughter, her Best Thing. That's what she used to call me. Best Thing. No contest. Poor Rob. I'll be sure he has my dad's number before Mom kicks him out.

# Chapter Four

Margaret says I'm starting to smell like macaroni and cheese. She says it's leaking out my pores. She says my skin has an orange tinge. Uh-huh. Right. She's just jealous because of my Very Own Cody Dillon Moment #2. Picture this: I'm alone in the art room, stuck washing out the brushes because I have a spare, and he comes in, all quiet and sneaky. He comes up behind me and puts his hands over my eyes. My heart's thumping because I'm thinking someone's playing a mean joke. But then I smell his cologne, but I'm not sure it's him because lots of the other guys copy him. He's not even supposed to be in the building, although he's not someone who'd be stopped by a stupid rule.

"Guess who?"

I shake my head because I really, really don't want to be wrong about this.

"C'mon. Guess."

I want to touch his hands, but my hands are wet, so that'd be nasty. I can feel his breath on my neck.

"Come on, Isabelle McAfferty," he says in that fake English accent. "You know exactly who this is."

It's him, and he knows my name. My whole name. "Cody Dillon?"

He keeps his hands over my eyes and puts his lips on my neck (LIPS

ON MY NECK!) and whispers in his regular voice, "That's right." He turns me around. His face is all serious. "Got anything to drop? I could pick it up for you."

I don't understand, so I shake my head, just as I realize he's referring to that time at the corner store. I consider dropping one of the brushes, but that part of the moment is over, so if I dropped something right now it would actually be lame.

"You're kind of cute, you know." (Margaret doesn't believe that part, but he said it. He really did. In his regular voice.)

My face goes hot and I say nothing because I am a complete mental gimp. He backs away. He stops at the door and points at me. "I got my eye on you," he says (HIS EYE ON ME!).

# Chapter Five

This is a Rob's-not-coming-home night. It's five in the morning. I can't sleep because even though I'm sure Rob the Slob is out screwing around, you never know, he might be bleeding to death in some car crash or something. I turn on the light and look in the mirror. Ugh. Cody Dillon has his eye on me, and I'm not worth having an eye on. That much is for sure.

I go to Mom and Rob's room and use the makeup she left behind. She taught me how to do it, and I've been watching her all my life. It's still hard to look good but not slutty. It takes me three tries to get the eyeliner right. Lipstick's easy. Blush is where you can go really wrong. Too much and you either look mentally ill or cheap. Too little and the rest of the makeup looks cheap. By the time I'm ready to leave for school, I'm looking pretty good if I do say so myself.

I borrow a pair of Mom's jeans. She says mine are too baggy. Hers are the kind that show your belly button if you wear the right kind of top. At first I put on her little T-shirt that says *kitten*, but it's too big in the chest because her tits are huge. I liked the way it showed my belly button, though. My tummy's nice and flat, not like Margaret's. Hers is doughy and lumpy. I hook a small gold hoop on my belly button, just to see what it looks like. Maybe when Mom comes back I'll ask if I can get my belly button pierced. I'll wait until after the blowout over Rob, though. I'll wait until she's feeling sorry for herself because she doesn't have a man, and then I'll ask and she'll say yes. She'll probably offer to do it with an ice cube and a sewing needle. I might let her, just to prove that I'm brave. Then again, I might not.

I take the shirt off and put on one of my own, the tightest I can find. I need a different bra. Sports bras make me look like mono-boob. I'll ask Rob for some money. He has to give it to me. It's Mom's money, and if he's pokered it all away by the time she comes home, there will be no question about which of us she picks. Mono-boob will have to do for now, though. Mom's bras are way too big.

# Chapter Six

I never see Cody Dillon with those two girls anymore. Margaret says they dropped out too. She says they're crackheads, living in some skanky apartment downtown. When I ask her how she knows that, she just says, "People."

"People, what?"

"People say."

She probably just overheard it in the bathroom. Margaret doesn't know people who would know that kind of thing. She could barely even say crack-head without wincing.

I put Mom's kitten shirt in the dryer a couple times and it shrinks enough for me to wear. That's what I'm wearing when I'm teaching Margaret how to smoke. We're hanging outside the corner store, and it's all dead boring until Cody Dillon drives by in his Jeep and waves while Margaret gracelessly hacks a lung out.

"Margaret! There he is! He just waved at me. Did you see that?"

Margaret recovers. "That shirt looks dumb, you know."

Okay, two can play this game.

"Dumb? Are you sure you're not jealous because you're too fat to wear a shirt like this?"

Her mouth gobs open. "Izzy?"

"Margaret?" I watch Cody Dillon drive away.

"Here, I don't want it." She hands me the cigarette and stomps off. She is fat. It's a fact.

I finish the cigarette and start another one. Cody Dillon drives by again. This time he stops.

"Come on. Get in."

Who's he talking to?

"Isabelle?"

That's me.

"Getting in?"

I climb in. It's so warm I get goosebumps. I was cold standing outside in the kitten shirt, but the only jacket I have is the babyish puffy one that makes me look chubby, when really I'm as skinny as you can get without being anorexic.

Cody Dillon puts his hand on my knee (HIS HAND ON MY KNEE!). "Want to go for a drive?"

I nod. He takes his hand off to shift gears. He can drive a standard. That's cool. His Jeep is cool. It's jacked up, with off-road tires and a skull with devil horns as the gearshift instead of a plain old knob.

"Where do you live?"

I tell him and he heads there. I pray Rob the Slob isn't home. His car is gone and Tuck is on his chain. Thank God.

"Whose dog?"

"Uh, mine, I guess."

We idle in the driveway. It starts raining. I don't want him to come in. The house is dirty, and all our stuff is old and rotten and lame and cheap and not even remotely cool.

"Aren't you going to ask me in?"

I shake my head. "We should probably go. My mom's boyfriend will be home soon and the last time I got caught skipping he kind of freaked out."

"Let's take the dog with us. He looks bored."

Tuck's sitting on the porch, staring at us. I let him off his chain. Cody Dillon whistles and Tuck leaps into the Jeep.

"In the back, boy," he says. Tuck hurls his big happy self into the back.

We drive to the river and walk along the railway tracks in the rain. We share a joint. Cody Dillon throws a stick for Tuck. It's like we're boyfriend-girlfriend, on a date. I wonder if his buddies dared him to do this. I wonder if I'm a bet. Does that make me a prize or a challenge? I don't want to ask. Either way, it feels good right this second. If right-this-second lasted forever, that would be okay by me. Margaret doesn't know what she's missing.

# Chapter Seven

Margaret and I hand out candy at my house on Halloween. Rob is at a poker game and isn't likely to come home. Margaret brings the candy because Rob still won't give me any money. I wrote Mom and ratted on him about him hoarding the money and not fixing the taps in the bathroom. The dripping is driving me mental. She called on the radiophone and told me I'm old enough to work things out without her. She has no idea the crap he pulls.

"Don't be a baby, Izzy," she said.

"I'm not! He's the one acting like a kid. Some nights he doesn't even—"

"Look, Izzy. I'm up here, you two are down there. Do me a favor and work it out. Okay?"

I'm working it out all right. Out of his wallet. Five dollars at a time, but only when he's won at poker and won't miss it. Cigarettes and tampons aren't exactly free. The last time I stole tampons, I almost got caught. I think the only reason the shop cop let me go was because he was embarrassed, or he felt sorry for me, or he's lazy, or all three.

Margaret says she'll buy me tampons. She says, "Wouldn't you just die if you got caught stealing tampons?" I tell her I don't want to talk about tampons on Halloween when there are bunches of little kids coming to the door looking all cute and innocent.

The trick-or-treating dies down about eight, and then it's just older losers, paper bags over their heads, or towel capes, maybe Dracula fangs or face paint if they're really trying. Very lame.

It's almost eleven. The lights are out. We're in our pajamas watching *Children of the Corn*, which we do every year. Margaret is scarfing down the leftover candy, which she does every year.

"You should stop, Margaret. It'll make your zits worse." She has a million zits, at least, all in various sizes and states of disgustingness. "And it's not going to help you lose weight, either."

"Yes, Mother."

"Do you want to be fat, Margaret?"

She scowls at me, ready to lecture me about how plumpness runs in her family, when the doorbell rings and Tuck starts barking. We sit up. Maybe it's because it's so late, or maybe it's the movie, but we're spooked.

"You go, Margaret."

"No, you go!"

"We'll both go," I say. We hold hands and creep to the door. I look through the spy hole. It's Cody Dillon, dressed as himself.

"Look!" I whisper.

Margaret looks. "Don't you dare open—"

I open the door. "Nice costume."

"Nice pajamas," he says. "Hi, Margaret."

"How do you know my name?" she asks.

"Isabelle talks about you."

"Isabelle?"

"That's what he calls me," I say. "Come in."

Cody Dillon is in my house (IN MY HOUSE!).

"Nobody has called her Isabelle since forever."

"I guess that makes me special, huh?" Cody Dillon is sitting on my couch (MY COUCH!). I wish it wasn't so skuzzy. I wish I had real clothes on. I wish Margaret would go away. Tuck gets up on the couch and stares at Cody Dillon with adoring droopy eyes.

"I love this movie," he says.

"What's he doing here?" Margaret whispers. "Did you invite him?"

I shake my head.

"Then tell him to leave!"

I shake my head again. Cody Dillon is rolling a joint in my living room (MY LIVING ROOM!). Margaret and I stare at him. He lights up and pats the couch. "Come sit beside me, Isabelle."

I sit beside him. Margaret stays by the door, arms crossed. Tuck stinks.

I wish I'd given him a bath. I pass the joint back to Cody Dillon.

Margaret shakes her head. "I'm going to bed."

Cody Dillon puts his arm across my shoulder (Um, hello, God? I believe in you as of right now) and we finish watching *Children of the Corn* together. When it's over, he does the following:

1. Pulls me onto his lap!

2. Puts his hands under my shirt and squeezes my mono-boob!

3. Kisses me, WITH TONGUE!

Then he's all cool, giving Tuck a little wrestle on the floor and then leaving like he comes over all the time and French kisses me and none of this is a big deal at all.

"See ya," he says, and then he's gone.

Margaret comes out and rewinds the tape to where she left in a huff.

"I was spying, you know."

"Then you saw him kiss me?"

"You better be careful." She turns the volume up. "He might have herpes or something."

"You're just jealous, Margaret Pritchard."

She pauses the movie and looks me straight in the eye. She's so serious it makes me giggle. "I am one hundred percent absolutely swear-on-my-father's-grave not jealous of you, Izzy McAfferty."

Whoa. She means it. She only swears on her father's grave for real. I watch her out of the corner of my eye. It looks like she's totally into the movie, but I think she's just pretending to watch it so she doesn't have to explain why she's not jealous. If she had to explain, she couldn't. I'm sure of it. I mean, come on, who wouldn't want to sit on Cody Dillon's lap? Well, Margaret, maybe. She is pretty heavy.

# Chapter Eight

The next time Cody Dillon finds me when I have a spare, we're just about out of the school when Mrs. Singh stops us. To look at her you wouldn't think she was a very scary principal; she's short and old and wears bright-colored saris that make her look cheerful to people who don't know any better.

"What was our agreement?" she says. I have no idea what she's talking about. I think back to the last time that I got caught skipping. There was no official agreement or anything, unless she means my promise not to ditch classes. "Do I need to bring out the contract you signed?"

Cody Dillon shakes his head. "No, ma'am."

"Good, now go." Mrs. Singh opens the fire door. Cody Dillon winks at me and then takes off across the field. Mrs. Singh lets the heavy door slam shut, the bang shuddering down the empty hall. She locks her hands behind her back and starts walking. I follow her, figuring we're headed to her office.

"I don't tend to give dating advice to my students," she says as we walk, "but I must say that you can do better for yourself, Izzy."

What am I supposed to say to that? She's just an old cow who doesn't know anything about me.

"I don't have time to sit with you and talk today," she says as we near the office. Inside, several important-looking people track her approach. "But I want you to know that if you ever want to talk, for any reason, my door is open, okay?"

I nod. What would be worse? A nice chat with her or my spider creep father?

The next day Cody Dillon comes and gets me for my spare, and we go out to his Jeep and smoke a joint. He says that old bag Singh made him sign a contract swearing he wouldn't set foot onto school property unless it was to arrange for his return as a student. I'm just about to ask him why he dropped out when he leans over and kisses me. We make out for a while and then smoke another joint.

That makes the afternoon all fuzzy and nice. I'm better at French when I'm high. My accent is flawless and I can figure out the verbs without trying very hard. Margaret won't talk to me when I'm high. She says I'm foggy and dumb and giggle too much, but really it's nice. The cool girls seem plastic and cheap when I'm high, and I don't stress out about what they think of me or that they whisper "white trash" under their breath when they pass me in the hall. When I'm high, I'm mellow, and nothing bothers me much.

It's a good thing I'm high when Mom shows up, unannounced. Margaret and I go to my house after school and there's Mom's car in the driveway. I can tell her about Cody Dillon, my boyfriend! I run into the house expecting hugs and kisses. There's Mom, on her knees, scrubbing the kitchen floor.

"You know, Izzy?" she says, no "hello'" or anything. "We might not have much, but we can take pride in what we do have." She rinses the rag in a bucket of grungy water. I see the kitchen in a new way. Not the let's-see-how-bad-it-gets-before-Rob-freaks-out way, but the Mom's-going-to-kill-me way. Moldy unwashed dishes in the sink, Tuck-hair everywhere, mystery gunk stuck in the spaghetti sauce on the floor that I never wiped up, dried egg like a giant smear of snot on the window from when Rob chucked one at me for lipping him off. There's even bits of shell stuck up there.

"Hi, Linda," Margaret says. "Want some help?"

"Go home, Margaret." She doesn't even look up. "Izzy is very grounded."

Margaret waves goodbye. I want to giggle. She looks so sad, like a little kid when a big kid snatches her favorite toy. Aw, c'mon, Mom, I want to say, it's not so bad. Hey, guess what, Mom? I have a BOYFRIEND! I sit at the kitchen table, chin on my hand.

"Well?" Mom throws the wet rag at me. It lands in my lap. I look like I've pissed my pants. If I wasn't stoned, I'd be furious. But it seems kind of funny. I grin.

"Wipe that look off your face and get busy, young lady."

"Yes, sir!"

"And take off my shirt." She glares at me. "What the hell do you think you're doing? Stealing my stuff? And get out of my jeans while you're at it!"

I change into my own clothes and go to help her, but she's decided she doesn't want my help. She sends me to my room, and I hear her muttering to herself, cursing me and Rob. When Rob comes home, the blowout I've been waiting for happens. It doesn't go the way I want it to.

"That little creep owes me over a hundred bucks!" he yells while she's ragging him out. "She's been stealing it right out of my wallet! What are you going to do about that, huh?"

Mom storms down the hall. I get ready to list all the crap Rob's pulled, starting with him not coming home some nights. My mother is a very jealous woman. Prepare for meltdown. She flings open the door.

"What the hell is wrong with you?"

Rob's behind her, arms crossed. Smug pig.

"He's cheating on you, Mom! He sometimes never even comes home!"

Mom whips around, nostrils flared. That's right, your turn, Rob the Slob. Arm thyself.

"What's she talking about?"

"Hey, whoa." Rob puts his hands up. "So I stay at one of the guy's houses now and again. You want me to drive drunk? The kid's looking for a way to come between us, babe. She's playing you. Can't you see that?"

"Izzy?"

"Mom! It's true!"

She's coming into my room now. This is very, very not good. She picks up an ashtray.

"Roaches?" She dumps the ashtray onto the floor. "You're buying drugs with my money?"

"My money," says Rob.

"Answer me, Izzy!"

I can't believe it. She's buying Rob's crap. I nod in total stunned disbelief, but she thinks I'm admitting to spending her money on pot when I really get it free from Cody Dillon, as much as I want, thank you very much.

"Get out!" she screams. "I can't believe the mess I come home to!"

"Aren't I very grounded?"

"You heard your mother," Rob says. "Get out!"

"Fuck off, Rob! This is all your fault!"

"Oh, that is it!" Mom yanks me up and drags me toward the bathroom. She thinks she's going to wash my mouth out with soap. Oh yeah? I don't think so. I tear away and run out of the house into the pouring rain. Tuck follows me. I keep running until I get to the gas station two blocks away. The guy grins all slimy at me when I ask to use the phone. He makes me beg before he lets me, the creep.

I call Cody Dillon's pager. I'm not allowed over at Margaret's anymore, not since her fat-cow mother blamed me for the missing booze and the cigarette burns on the carpet, even though it was both of us. Well, maybe it was mostly me, but still.

Cody Dillon comes and rescues me (RESCUES ME!). He takes me to his apartment (HIS OWN APARTMENT!) and runs me a bubble bath. He lights a bunch of candles and turns the light off. He sits on the floor and keeps me company. He says I can stay here as long as I want. Um, hello, heaven? Izzy McAfferty has arrived, in case anyone wants to know.

# Chapter Nine

After we have sex for the first time, Cody Dillon tells me it's okay to just call him Dillon.

"That's what my friends call me." He passes me the joint.

I'm really hurting, and there's blood, but he pretends not to notice, which is sweet of him. I lied and told him it wasn't my first time, so he wouldn't think I was a prude, but oh my God did it ever hurt! I smile at him and sit up. Tuck is lying in the doorway. I wonder if he watched the whole time. That makes my stomach flip. Gross.

"Go away, Tuck!" He slinks off, tail between his legs.

"That was your first time, wasn't it?" Cody Dillon, just Dillon, I guess, puts a hand on my naked knee. I would like him to remove it.

I nod.

He squeezes my knee.

"I thought so. It gets better, trust me." He kisses my knee. "You need to shave your legs, babe."

I pull the sleeping bag over my legs. "Sorry."

"That's okay." He takes the joint. "I'll buy you what you need. Let's go shopping."

We drive into the city, to the big mall downtown. Dillon buys me a whole set of new clothes, expensive, tight-fitting, cool stuff that supermodels wear.

"You're built like a model," he says. "Only, you're a little short. Still, you're hot."

"My tits are too small," I say. "I'm too skinny." (HE SAYS I'M HOT!).

He pinches my scrawny butt. "Skinny's good. You can always buy bigger tits."

Not including all the clothes, he buys me the following:

1. Four new bras, all the padded push-up kind, all black and slinky.

2. Sexy black knee-high boots that zip up the sides.

3. Brand new makeup, the complete works, all good quality and EXPENSIVE!

4. A cell phone (MY VERY OWN CELL PHONE!).

We sit in the food court and eat Chinese food and he shows me how to use the cell phone. There are all kinds of rings to choose from. I pick "Someday My Prince Will Come," but he says, "I'm right here, babe," and he's right, so I change it. Now it meows when I get a call.

This skank comes up to our table. She's a little older than me, but not much, maybe sixteen or seventeen. She's all dolled up, but she's got scabs on her face, so it makes the dolled-up stuff look really nasty.

"Dillon?"

Dillon ignores her.

"You got five bucks or something?"

"I'm busy, go away." Dillon winks at me.

"C'mon, Dillon. Just five bucks. I can't wait until next week."

Dillon takes a five off the wad of cash he was spending on me and gives it to her. "Scram, Erin."

She scrams, right away, without even saying thanks.

"Dumb crackhead," Dillon says.

"How do you know her?"

Dillon shrugs. "My buddy's girlfriend."

"Oh." I don't want my chow mein anymore. Something about the girl turned me off. Her smell maybe, cheap perfume and seriously bad body funk. "She stinks."

"Forget about her." Dillon takes my hands in his. "Today is all about you."

When we get back to Dillon's place, I phone Margaret to tell her about all my new stuff. She's not home. Her fat-cow mother says she's with "her nice new friend," but she won't tell me where they are. I bet they're at Teen Night at the rec center. This new friend, Amanda, is her science lab partner. She doesn't smoke pot or cigarettes, doesn't drink, not even a little, and has never stolen anything in her life, not even a jawbreaker from the corner store. Margaret's mother loves Amanda. Amanda loves Teen Night. Her older sister first organized it, and now Amanda is sort of half in charge. Margaret says she only goes for the free chips and pop, but I know better. She likes the "in-charge" part and she likes the geeky movies they watch and she likes that her mother thinks Amanda is a "nice new friend," rather than a "saucy little tart," which is what she's thought of me since I was eight.

Dillon goes out later, and after about five minutes I get bored. His apartment only has one room besides the kitchen and the bathroom. There's not even a TV.

I try to read his 4x4 magazines, but they're so boring they make me sleepy. I smoke a joint because there's nothing else to do. I decide right now is a good time to try Margaret again. She answers on the first ring.

"It's after midnight, Izzy!"

"Is Amanda there?"

"No."

"Don't lie. She is too, isn't she?"

"Okay, so she is. So what?"

I shrug, even though she can't see. "I was just going to tell you something." I look over at my new stuff. I should put it away, but I like the way the boxes and bags look all together, like a hotel porter brought them in.

"So tell me."

"I changed my mind. I don't want to tell you anymore."

There's a pause. I bet that priss Amanda is mouthing something at her.

"Are you mad at me, Izzy?"

I'm not mad. I'm high. I never get mad when I'm high. But I'm done. I'm done with Margaret.

"Ding."

Margaret says, "What?"

"Ding! You're done, Margaret."

"Are you high?"

"Ding!" I say. "Whoops, better take you out of the oven!" I hang up.

I paint my fingernails ten different colors. I paint my toenails ten different colors. I clean it all off and paint them all black. I try on all my new clothes and try out all the new makeup. I'm buzzing. I wonder if there's something extra in the pot. I turn the lights out and try to relax. At first I can't sleep, and then all of a sudden I'm out.

Dillon wakes me up. I fell asleep in the sexy boots and leather mini-skirt and nothing else. He's brought a friend home. The friend is grinning down at me. I yank the sleeping bag over me.

His name is Barrel, and he's big and round like one.

"She'll do," he says. Then he leaves.

"Do what?" My head is pounding.

"Nothing. Don't worry about it." Dillon heads for the shower. "Go back to sleep."

So I do.

# Chapter Ten

My mom calls my cell the day she's heading back to camp.

"You doing okay?"

"Yeah."

"Margaret's mom taking good care of you?"

"Sure."

"Well..." I hear a zipper. Is she getting dressed? Doing up a bag?

"Well, I've been thinking, Izzy. Just until my contract's done—"

"I can't come home?" I don't even want to go home, but I want to cry anyway. "Is that what you're saying?"

"No, baby. Not at all. I just wondered if you'd rather stay at Margaret's than come back here and bicker with Rob all the time I'm gone, you know?"

I nod. Rob the Slob. I can't believe she picked him over her Best Thing.

"Izzy? Baby?"

"Yeah, Mom."

"So how about I give Margaret's mom some money and you stay put until I get back?"

"Mrs. Pritchard already told me she'd never take money from us. She knows we don't have any, and besides, she says parenting isn't a paying job." This hurts, I can tell by Mom's sudden intake of breath and the silence that follows. Good. It was meant to. "She says I can stay for as long as I want. She said that. As long as I want. Like, till I graduated if I wanted."

"Oh." I hear a tap running. Is she in the kitchen? "Hey, Izzy, about the money you stole from Rob..."

I wait. "Yeah?"

"He won't let me pay him back for it. He says you stole it, so you pay it back from your own money. He totaled it up. He says you owe him two hundred dollars."

"It wasn't that much!"

"But you did steal it, right?"

"Not that much!"

"I'm not going to argue about the amount. Maybe this'll teach you a lesson."

I hang up on her. She calls back. The phone meows. I don't answer. I answer later, though, because I'm waiting for Dillon to come home and I think it's him. It's Mom.

"Don't you hang up on me! I'm just about to get on the plane. I wanted to tell you Rob says you can come home when you've got the two hundred dollars."

"What if you send me the money and I'll say it's mine?"

"Can't, baby. This is your mess. You got to clean it up this time."

I hear an airplane taking off. A baby crying. A boarding announcement for a flight to Calgary. I wish I was getting on the plane with her, like when I was little and I got to go to camp with her. I used to play in the cupboards under the counter. I'd make one a fort, with blankets and pillows, a stash of cookies, books to read and a flashlight. The cupboards were metal, and my voice echoed. I used to lie in the dark and sing to myself, just to hear the echo. I liked being a little kid, but that was a long time ago.

# Chapter Eleven

Barrel brings over a Chinese girl named Kitty. She's even skinnier than me, but has bigger tits. She and I sit on the mattress in the other room and paint each other's nails while Dillon and Barrel take the only chairs into the kitchen, shut the door and talk in low voices. I tell Kitty about my mom's kitten shirt.

"I'd give it to you." I'm having a hard time getting the polish on neat. I've had too much coffee and too much pot and too much beer and there's no food around to take the edge off. "I will give it to you, when I can go home and get it."

"Thanks, but it's okay." She has an accent, even though she was born in Richmond. I want to ask her to say something in Chinese, but I'm worried that'd be racist. "I got a couple of shirts like that. And some underwear."

"Here, look." I make my cell phone meow. She loves it, so we set hers to do the same.

"Is Barrel your boyfriend?"

Kitty laughs, dripping a splotch of polish on my foot. She wipes it off. "Barrel?" She lowers her voice. "Gross. He's not my boyfriend."

"Then how do you know him?"

Dillon and Barrel come into the room. Dillon leans against the wall, arms crossed. Barrel snatches Kitty's arm and yanks her up.

"Let's go."

"Hey!" I grab her other arm. "Don't grab her like that!"

Kitty winks at me. "It's okay, Izzy."

I let go of her. "It doesn't look okay to me."

"That's what I mean," Barrel says to Dillon. "You keep an eye on that."

Barrel frowns at me. His clothes might be expensive and nice, but they're all a little small on him and have the sheen of not being washed in a very long time. He looks swollen, like he might burst out of them. He probably thinks he looks muscular, but he just looks bloated. I bite back a smirk.

"What?" He shoves Kitty toward the door and hauls me up by my arm. "Wipe that look off your face, slut!"

That's funny. Yeah, that's me, Little Miss Sleep Around. I know I shouldn't, but I really want to laugh right in his chubby face. My smirk grows. He smacks me. I fall back onto the mattress, not because of the force—it wasn't that hard, really—but I was so surprised. Good old Tuck, he doesn't even wake up, let alone race to my rescue.

"Hey! Dillon?" Dillon stays where he is and shakes his head. "Do something, Dillon!" I scream. "He hit me!"

Barrel glares down at me, his sweaty cheeks flushed. Behind him, Dillon puts a shut-up finger to his lips. Kitty shakes her head and mouths "don't." She presses something on her phone and it meows.

The sound surprises Barrel. He whips around and then realizes it's just a phone. Stupid me wants to laugh again, at the thought that a cat could startle Big Bad Barrel. Don't laugh, Izzy. Bad idea.

"Yeah. Yeah, okay." Kitty talks into the phone. "Okay. Ten minutes. No problem." She hangs up. Barrel gets his keys out of his pocket.

"Where?"

"Franklin and Gower."

Kitty winks at me as Barrel gives me one last glare. He pushes her out ahead of him and slams the door. When they've gone, Dillon tells me Kitty is Barrel's drug mule. He's the dealer, but he gets Kitty to carry the drugs because he has a criminal record and she doesn't and she's underage and he's not. If she gets caught, she probably won't get charged at all, or if she did, her record would get wiped when she turns nineteen. It actually kind of makes sense.

Dillon is still leaning against the wall. His eyes are closed now.

"Do you love me, Isabelle?"

Tuck wakes up; it's that shocking a question. Of course I do!

"Of course, Dillon!"

His eyes are still closed. "You'd do anything for me?"

My skin goes a little cold, or hot, I can't tell. It's his tone. So sad. So tired.

I nod, but his eyes are closed, so he can't see me. It takes a while to find my voice.

"Yeah." I wait for him to ask me to mule for him, or Barrel, but he doesn't.

When Dillon opens his eyes, he looks out the grimy window and not at me. I said I'd wash them, and I still haven't. I get a bottle of vinegar and an old newspaper and start cleaning the windows. Dillon stares past me. It's raining outside. The cars whoosh by on the wet road. I wipe the glass hard, squeaky clean. The streetlights come on. It gets dark so early now.

"What's wrong, Dillon?"

He shakes his head. "Nothing for you to worry about."

He lights a cigarette and lies down on the mattress. What if a fire starts like that? What if Dillon dies? I'm gripped by panic, grief, terror at the thought of losing him. I must love him. That's what love is, isn't it? I can't believe my mom feels this way about Rob the Slob. She can't really be in love with him, not like I am with Dillon.

"Dillon?"

He's fallen asleep. I take the cigarette from his fingers and cover him with the sleeping bag. I go into the kitchen and wash the window in there and then the counters and the fridge and the floor. I'm on the floor in the bathroom, scrubbing, when Dillon comes in to pee.

"Maybe you could get a job," he says.

"Is it money?" I sit on the edge of the bathtub. It needs cleaning too. And the toilet. "Is that what's wrong?"

"Well, you're living here for free, right?" He leans in the doorway.

I nod.

"Someone would pay you to do this work, you know."

I go back to scrubbing the floor. Yes, I am living here for free, but here I am on my hands and knees, trying to make up for it! I'm mad, but then I think, I'm not mad—I'm in love, and sometimes things are rough in love. But it's worth it.

"Nah," Dillon says. "You'd get crap money."

I don't answer. I'm afraid if I do I'll sound lippy, and he's so stressed out, I don't want to set him off. He's trying. I know that. He really is.

"Look, Isabelle." My heart warms a little when he says my name. "I'll think of something. Don't you worry about it, okay?"

I dry my hands and put my arms around him. "Will you tell me if I can do anything?"

He nods, kisses the top of my head. I would do anything to be with him, anything to not have to go home to Rob the Slob.

## Chapter Twelve

Margaret corners me in front of the school as soon as Dillon pulls away in his Jeep, with Tuck sitting pretty in the front seat like he's always been Dillon's dog.

"Where have you been?"

"Dillon's. You know that."

Margaret rolls her eyes. Amanda is standing off to the side, pretending not to be listening. She's so obvious.

"Why haven't you been at school?"

I shrug. "I'm here now."

She rolls her eyes again. She glances at Amanda. Amanda purses her lips.

"Yeah, but what about the last three weeks?"

"It hasn't been that long!"

Amanda purses her lips tighter and adds an annoying rise to her eyebrows. She looks like she's about to birth a toad out of her mouth. "Oh, yes it has."

"Stay out of it, Amanda." If I were someone different, I'd punch her prissy lights out right about now.

"We're worried about you, Izzy." Margaret's expression is so sweet, I wish I could ignore the "we," but I can't.

"We?"

Margaret pales. "Well, of course Amanda is worried about you too. Right, Amanda?" Amanda nods so enthusiastically that I wouldn't be surprised if her head fell right off and rolled into traffic.

"What the hell does she care?" I glare at Amanda. She smiles like I'm some kind of gimp to pity.

"Of course I care." Amanda's breath stinks. Good luck ever trying to find a man who'll kiss that.

I shake my head. "I don't need this crap."

Margaret takes my hand. "Mrs. Singh's been asking about you."

"Did you give her my number?" If she did, I'll kill her.

Margaret looks like I've slapped her. "How could I?" She lowers her voice, but that just makes Amanda perk up her ears. "You never gave it to me, Izzy."

"Well, Margaret..." God, some friend I am. "You never asked."

"Come on, Margaret." Amanda backs away. "We've got to get to class."

Margaret stares at me for a second and then follows Amanda inside.

It gets worse. Mrs. Singh takes me out of my first class and escorts me straight to her office. I actually love her office; it smells like oranges and cloves, and it's decorated with Indian tapestries and rugs and shimmering blue and gold drapes. She is the first East Indian principal in the district, and only the third woman ever. Last year, the news was right into her and she gave television interviews in this office, dressed in her saris. My mom says she's glamorous and smart, but what does that matter if you hate kids? Everybody knows she hates kids.

There's a bowl of East Indian sweets on her desk, but you're only allowed one if you're in there because of something good. She takes one, tucking it into the corner of her mouth to speak. "Tell me, Izzy."

"Tell you what?"

She rolls her hands in front of her. "Come on, tell me." She has a real English accent mixed in with her East Indian accent. It sounds like a nice smell. She should work at some posh private school where everyone's polite and wears uniforms, not this grungy hole. I wonder why she doesn't?

"Okay, fine, Izzy."

Fine, what?

"You leave me no choice."

I sit up. I know where this is going, and I don't like it one bit. "But I've been sick!"

She laughs. I can see the sweet at the back of her mouth.

"Is that right?"

I nod. My nice long polished nails find their way to my teeth. I start gnawing.

"I'll be honest with you, Izzy. I don't believe you. Not even one little bit."

I shrug.

"I'm suspending you for three days."

"But I just got back!"

"Over the next three days, I want you to think seriously about the direction of your life. Come to me first thing Thursday morning and we will make a plan together."

"For what?"

"One plan for you to stay in school and another plan to deal with your drug problem. The two plans will work together."

"News flash, lady. I don't have a drug problem!"

Mrs. Singh pushes the bowl of sweets to me. Maybe they're for lost-hope cases too. I don't want one now, even though the licorice smell makes my mouth water.

"That will be all, Miss McAfferty." She pops another sweet into her mouth.

"I will see you first thing Thursday morning. In the meantime, your job is to think hard about where you want to go in life and how you will get there."

Margaret is waiting for me in the hall.

"What happened?"

"Leave me alone, Margaret." I bee-line for the front doors, hoping to make it outside before I start to cry. I've never been suspended before. It feels awful, worse than getting caught stealing. Margaret runs along beside me.

"Tell me what happened!"

I push out the front doors; she's still following me.

"Look, Margaret, buzz off, okay? Go find your girlfriend."

Margaret folds her arms. "You're being mean, Izzy."

"And you're just plain immature. Grow up a bit, and then maybe we'll have something in common. In the meantime, go play tea party and dolls with Amanda."

Margaret slowly backs away, turning at the last moment before she disappears inside. I stand on the sidewalk, stuck. I want to run after her and apologize, but I also just want to run away and never see her again. I stand there until Mrs. Singh comes out with her coat on, a purple scarf at her throat. She's carrying a briefcase, her car keys in the other hand.

"Is there a problem, Izzy?"

That seems like such a simple question, yet I don't have even the start of an answer. I shake my head and start walking toward Dillon's place. He'll make it all better. He'll know what to do.

# Chapter Thirteen

Dillon says I'm crazy not to think that being suspended is great.

"Three days off? Enjoy them!"

He's mad about my chewed-up nails though. We go over to Barrel's house so Kitty can fix them. More people come over, and soon it's a party and I don't care that we're at Big Bad Barrel's because I'm having a great time.

His place is so much nicer. It's a whole house and the stereo is huge and there's lot's of comfy places to curl up and chill out when I get tired of dancing. Dillon likes it when I dance. All the guys like it. There are lots of guys.

"Get her to dance again!" That's Martin. He always wears a suit. He keeps nipping into the bathroom. I don't know who he thinks he's fooling. We all know he's doing drugs in there. He's not very good at sharing.

Dillon pulls me off the couch. It's dark outside. We've been here all day. I feel like my wineglass is welded to my hand. It keeps getting filled and emptied and filled and emptied. I'm doing the emptying, but I don't know who's doing the filling.

Dillon stands me up in the middle of the room. I teeter a little, but try not to. It's these high heels. I take them off and throw them at Martin because he's looking at me funny. He catches them and laughs.

That's better. Not so tippy. I want to seem like I can handle myself. I don't want to look like some drunken floozy mess, even though that's exactly what I am at the moment. Oh well. You live once, right?

Dillon lifts my arms over my head and Martin pulls my shirt off. I'm wearing one of the black push-up bras. Martin wolf-whistles. I drape my arms over Dillon's shoulders, but he pushes me away.

"No, babe. By yourself."

Barrel turns up the stereo and I dance, spinning and spinning until I feel sick. I lunge for the bathroom, but Martin's in there again. I puke on Barrel's brand-new leather chair, the one that matches the couch and the stool. Barrel calls it an ottoman, just to sound posh.

I try to wipe it off, but Barrel sees. I wait for him to come and give me hell.

He comes over, but doesn't rough me up at all. He rubs my back.

"I'll just add that to the tab." He winks and walks away.

I wish he'd come back and rub my back some more. I call for Dillon. Maybe he'll come and rub my back. Kitty tells me he left.

"With Erin."

That skank from the mall? I lurch to the front door. Tuck and Dillon and the Jeep are gone. I crawl upstairs and fall asleep on an enormous, soft bed. It's just getting light out when I wake up. Martin is asleep beside me. His suit is still on, but his fly is open. I'm sure nothing happened. But I'm naked, so I'm not that sure. If anything did happen, it's my fault for being such a drunken slut. I pull on my skirt and bra. I can't find my underwear. Bad sign. Where's my shirt?

I find my shirt and my shoes in the living room. Kitty is asleep on the couch, spooned with a skinny man with a goatee. I think he was the one that brought out the coke. I didn't do any, I don't think. I wonder where Barrel is?

It's snowing, great big fat flakes. They're melting when they land, but it's too cold to go back to Dillon's like this. I take a sweater from the floor. I think it's Kitty's. I'll give it back. I pass the leather chair I puked on. It's badly stained.

I walk across town in my teetery heels. Some jerk-off in a pickup slows beside me and offers me a ride. I know what he's after. I'm not that stupid. If only Dillon was here.

"My boyfriend would beat the crap out of you if he was here." I look at his license plate, but my head's too foggy to remember the number.

"Oh, your boyfriend, huh?" The man is older than Barrel, close to Rob's age. He looks familiar, but maybe that's because all slobby creeps look the same.

"Yeah. That's right, my boyfriend."

He laughs. "Whatever you say, sweetheart." He drives off. I give him the finger.

Do I still have a boyfriend? Did I cheat on him? He wouldn't dump me for scabby-faced Erin, would he?

I stand outside Dillon's door for a minute before I knock. He hasn't given me a key yet. He keeps forgetting to get another one cut. There's no answer. Maybe he's not there. His Jeep isn't. Or maybe he's just pretending not to be there. Maybe he's in there with Erin. I pound harder. No answer.

"Tuck?" If he's in there, I'll at least hear his tags jingle. I whistle. "Here, boy!"

Nothing.

I have nowhere else to go, so I go home and wait in the shed until Rob finally leaves. I go in through the basement window that doesn't lock. I have a hot shower and then make myself the biggest meal I've had since I moved in with Dillon: bacon, eggs, toast and a stack of pancakes drenched with syrup and butter. I page Dillon every ten minutes or so. He doesn't call. He's dumped me. I know it. I don't blame him. I wait for Rob to come home and plan how I'll beg to be allowed to stay.

# Chapter Fourteen

Rob freaks out that I'm even in the house at all, so no, I'm not allowed to stay. He says I should be happy he's not going to call the cops and have me arrested for break and enter. He says when I do come back with the money I stole, I damned well better bring his dog back too. That's going to be harder than getting together two hundred dollars.

I can't imagine Dillon giving up Tuck. They go everywhere together now.

I go to the mall and page Dillon a million times. He never calls. I go back to Barrel's. Thank God only Kitty and another couple of girls are there. She says Barrel and Dillon took Erin to Kelowna to work. Personally, I think Erin would make a really bad drug mule. She seems stunned most of the time. I think she's into heroin, but I don't want to know, so I don't ask. There are marks on her arms, though. If I find out Dillon ever slept with her, I'll make him get tested for STDs. Mind you, if anything happened with me and that Martin creep, I should probably get tested too. Oh, so gross.

Kitty's letting me stay until Dillon and Barrel get back. She lends me some pajamas and we stay in all day and watch soap operas and talk shows. The other girls sleep all day and only come downstairs on their way out after dark.

"Where are they going?" It's snowing harder and is sticking to the ground now.

"Work."

"Where do they work?"

Kitty rolls her eyes. "At an all-night dry cleaners, you idiot."

How was I supposed to know that? Kitty says I can sleep in the big bed, but that's the one I woke up with Martin in and it gives me the creeps. I sleep on the couch in the living room instead.

In the morning, I get cleaned up for my meeting with Mrs. Singh. I get almost to the front doors of the school before it dawns on me. The school is very closed.

I actually think this: Why would Mrs. Singh tell me to meet her on

Thursday if she knew full well that there was no school today? I actually think this too: Does Mrs. Singh really hate kids that much?

Only the doors to the gym are open. A woman is shouting over some canned music.

"And one! And two!"

I peek in. It's an exercise class. Oh my God, there's Margaret! She's sweating. The fat on her thighs jiggles. Those shorts are too short, really. Amanda is beside her, slender and really very coordinated, I have to say. The rest of the class is all fat women, including the instructor. She's at the front, her back to the mirrored wall. Amanda catches sight of me in the mirror. She locks eyes with me and doesn't miss a step. I wait for her to poke Margaret. I wait for Margaret to come and tell me off in that reassuring, self-righteous way that she has. Amanda smiles like an ice queen and looks away.

Margaret is busy trying to keep up. She doesn't look away from the instructor, not even once. I back away.

There's a sign on the bulletin board beside the door. *Saturday morning fat-to-fit classes 8–10 am.* Saturday? It absolutely cannot be Saturday.

Kitty confirms it. The party lasted three days, didn't I know that? I ask her how I ended up sharing a bed with Martin.

"Oh, you mean Reg."

"Is that his name? The guy in the suit?"

"No, Reg was the one wearing black track pants."

"Martin," I say. "The guy in the suit." But I can almost remember a pair of black track pants. There were snaps down the sides. I push the memory out of the way. "His name is Martin."

"Oh, him. Uh, hey..." Kitty pours milk into a pot and puts it on to heat. "I think the guys will be back tomorrow."

I hope she doesn't mean Martin and the track pants guy. "Dillon?"

She nods. She takes out a big ceramic bowl and dumps a bag of flour in it.

"What are you doing?" I know she's changed the subject from the party. She probably doesn't want to embarrass me. I'm okay with that, especially because I don't want to know about me and Reg, if there is anything to know about me and Reg. So long as Dillon never knows about any of it. Not that anything actually happened. At least, I hope not. If it did, I pray Martin was too screwed up to remember. As for this Reg guy, I'm just going to pretend Kitty never even brought him up.

"I'm making bread." She adds the hot milk to the flour, yeast and sugar.

"For Barrel?"

She laughs. "No. For myself."

I imagine Kitty learned to make bread from her mother, or maybe her grandmother. I imagine them speaking Chinese together in the kitchen. I imagine Kitty as a little girl in Chinese slippers and a satin quilted jacket, standing on a chair, beaming up at her beautiful mother.

"Are you making Chinese bread? The kind your mother made?"

"My mother make bread?" Kitty laughs again. "No, I learned it from a book."

For some reason that makes me so sad I almost cry. We watch TV while the dough rises, and then more TV when the bread is baking. My mouth waters when she takes it out of the oven. We sit on the counter and wait for it to cool a little, and then we eat the whole loaf, slathering on butter and apricot jam.

When the other girls wake up and come downstairs, they say we'll get fat from all that bread. They pour themselves cups of coffee and take them with them when a car pulls up out front and honks its horn.

"Why do they dress like that if they work at a dry cleaners?"

Kitty lets me have the last piece of bread. She shakes her head.

"Honey, they don't work at a dry cleaners. I was being sarcastic. They're hookers."

I wait a little too long before I answer, so I doubt she believes me.

"I knew that." I just can't bear to admit that I was that naïve. I can't believe I called Margaret immature when I'm such a stupid baby myself! "I knew they were hookers. I was just being funny."

"You and Dillon should have a talk when he comes home."

"A talk about what?" Maybe he knows about Martin already. Maybe one of the girls told him. Maybe Kitty knows something I don't know. Maybe Martin paid for me. Maybe Reg did. Maybe there were more! I tell myself it's about the leather chair. The other girls moved it onto the porch because it stank. It's even more ruined now that it got snowed and rained on.

"You ever heard of roofies?" Kitty says.

I shake my head.

"It's a date-rape drug." She cleans up the mess on the table like she's talking about the weather and not about something scary. "I think someone put it in your drink. How else can you explain losing three whole days?"

I can't go to the cops. Dillon would be furious. No one would believe me. It probably wasn't that at all. It was just stupid me, being a drunken skank. I deserved it. From now on, though, I'll make sure I know who's topping up my drink.

"Nothing happened."

"You're probably right," Kitty says.

# Chapter Fifteen

Dillon doesn't even say hello when he and Barrel get back. He steers me into the Jeep and we go straight to his place.

"We gotta talk." He knows about Martin, I know it. "I'm in trouble, Isabelle."

He's in trouble? I think about Kelowna. What did he do?

"Is it Erin?"

"Who?"

"The girl you took to Kelowna? I'm not mad about it. She was with Barrel, right?" Besides, who am I to talk? Waking up with Martin the suited creepster, never mind the three days I can't remember at all.

He laughs. "You think I cheated on you with her?"

I say nothing. He starts pacing.

"I love you. I'd never cheat on you!" I want to die. He's so good to me and I'm such a skank! "I mean trouble," he says. "BIG trouble."

I start to get scared. "What did you do?"

"Me?" He stops pacing. "Oh, this isn't about me."

I know what he's going to say. "This is about you, Isabelle." I was right. It is about Martin. And Reg. And who knows what else. Only, it's not.

"Barrel's my dealer, okay?"

I knew that. "And?"

"And it's time to pay up."

I scoot back on the mattress until my back is against the wall. "What do you mean?"

"We've been together for three months, right?"

Over three months now. For our three-month anniversary, he took me out to an expensive Italian restaurant in the city. We stayed at a motel, even, and sneaked Tuck in so he didn't have to sleep in the Jeep.

"You know what three months adds up to when you party as much as you?"

"I don't smoke any more than you do, Dillon."

Dillon sits on the mattress. He lights a cigarette and doesn't offer me one.

"Yeah, but when it was just me, I could afford it." He sounds sad. "The work I do for Barrel, that pays for me to keep this place. He gives me pot and booze as a bonus, kind of. You know what I mean?"

"Yeah."

He shakes his head. I put my hands on his back. He shakes his head again.

"When we were in Kelowna..."

He stops. I scoot around so I'm sitting in front of him. I put my hands on his shoulders.

"What, honey? What happened?"

"Nothing happened. It's what he said. I had no idea." Dillon gets up and starts pacing again. "I owe him five thousand dollars, Isabelle."

"No." I cover my mouth with my hands and shake my head. "Oh, no."

He nods. "He says I have until Friday to get him the money or he'll send his boys after me."

I've heard of these boys. I've never met them, but Kitty has. She saw them beat up some scrawny kid who owed

Barrel a couple of hundred dollars. What would they do for five thousand?

"I'm in real trouble here." Dillon looks like he's about to cry. That's not what he does. He doesn't cry. That's not Dillon. "I need to get a job, something, anything!"

"No job will pay that much that fast!"

It's all my fault. If I hadn't stolen the money from Rob, I wouldn't have been kicked out, I wouldn't be leaching off Dillon, and he wouldn't owe Big Bad Barrel five thousand dollars.

"I know," he whispers. "But what can I do?"

I steer him to a chair in the kitchen and look in the fridge. I want to make him something to eat, or a hot drink, but there's nothing. "Do you want a glass of water?"

He shakes his head. "I need a lot more than a glass of water, babe."

I sit down. "What can I do?"

"Nothing." He puts his head in his hands. "Nothing. No. Never."

"Tell me." I grip his wrists. "I love you, Dillon."

"And I love you," he says. "Which is why I told him no way."

And then I get it. Yeah, maybe some of the girls mule for Barrel and his boys, but the others, like the two hookers at Barrel's house, they work for Barrel. Barrel is a pimp. Those girls are Barrel's girls, just like Kitty probably is, and now he wants me too. "No!" I shake my head. "I won't do it!"

"That's right, you won't. And I'd never let you."

"I'm not like those other girls."

"That's right! You're not." He kisses my forehead, my cheeks, my lips. "You're mine."

We sit in the kitchen as it gets darker. I get up to turn the light on.

It doesn't work. I look in the cupboard for a lightbulb.

"It's not the lightbulb," Dillon says. "We got cut off. Maybe it's time for you to go home."

"I can't!" He wouldn't let me take Tuck and I don't have two hundred dollars and Mom's not back for another couple of months and what would happen to him? I got him into this. I can't just walk away knowing he's in trouble. I shake my head. "I won't leave you."

Dillon says something, but so quietly I can't hear him. "What?"

"I was saying what if? You know, you'd just have to do it a couple of times, and then we'd be square and we can forget it ever happened."

"With Barrel?" My stomach flips. I can't. I'd be sick. I'm going to be sick at just the thought of it!

"At first." Dillon stares at his shoes. It's too dark for me to see his face. He sounds defeated. Lost. Helpless. "You know, that five thousand doesn't even include the chair."

The chair. The brand-new leather chair that me, myself and I ruined all by myself.

"It doesn't?" My legs begin to tremble. "How much do I owe him?"

"Two thousand for the chair." There's a catch in his voice. "Do you know about Barrel's boys?"

"Yes," I whisper.

"Do you have any idea what they'll do to me?"

I shake my head.

"They'll probably kill me, Isabelle. Seven thousand dollars." He gets up. "Think about it."

We lie on the mattress in the cold dark, the sleeping bag and our coats covering us. He holds me. We say nothing. He falls asleep first and I watch his breath in the frosty air. I fall asleep hours later, but I only sleep for a few moments at a time because of that awful nightmare I keep having, the one about me and Martin in the bed, only he's wearing black track pants with snaps down the sides instead of his suit. I stay awake by pinching the skin at my wrist whenever I feel myself drifting off. By morning I have made my decision. I'll do it. If it will keep Dillon safe, alive, I'll do it. Sometimes you just have to do terrible things. No one ever said love was easy. No one ever said life was easy either.

# Chapter Sixteen

Dillon said he couldn't even be in the same town while it was happening. He was so torn up about it that when I was getting ready to go to Barrel's, he put his fist through the wall. His fist was swollen badly. I wrapped some ice from the 7-Eleven in a dishtowel and made him sit at the table and stay put before he could hurt himself any more.

"I know this is hard," I said. "It'll all be over soon."

He buried his face in my stomach. "It's just that I love you so much!"

"I love you too, Dillon."

Then Barrel's car arrived, driven by one of his boys.

I waited for Dillon to kiss me goodbye, but he didn't. I understand; it's all so weird and gross right now.

I manage not to be sick while it's happening, but right after Barrel leaves the room I make a dash for the bathroom and stay in there for almost an hour, retching. At least I didn't get any of it on anything expensive.

After I've been in the bathroom for a couple of minutes, Barrel sends Kitty in. She rubs my back and coos nice things at me about how it's all okay, and that's just how life goes.

"He sent you in here to make me feel better?" I wipe my face.

She shrugs. "You really want to know?"

I nod.

"He sent me in to make sure you don't escape." She raises her eyes to the tiny window above the toilet. We're in the upstairs bathroom.

"I'd break my legs!" I sound alarmed, but it's only a couple of seconds later before I consider whether or not that would be any worse than being stuck under the great big heaving, hairy weight of Barrel, Lord King of Disgustingness and All That Is Revolting.

She shrugs. "Some have."

"Some?" I start crying again. "How many?"

She rubs my back some more. "Just take care of yourself, okay?"

"That's what you do? Take care of yourself?" I push her hand away. "Is that why you never told me?"

She shrugs again. “Stop shrugging!” I scream. There’s a knock at the door. It’s one of Barrel’s boys.

“Everything okay?”

“It’s fine,” Kitty chirps. She pushes my hair out of my face and whispers, “Knowing what you know now, do you blame me?”

I shake my head. I don’t know what I would’ve done if I was in her position.

“So, if you know what’s good for you, you’ll do the same.”

“Or what?”

She starts to shrug again. She catches herself and grins. “How about I make you some bread?”

When she says that, she becomes old. She becomes the grandmother I’ve never had. She puts on seventy-five years like it’s a comfy old housecoat. She looks tired and hopeful and safe. She pats my puffy cheeks.

"Have a shower. It'll make you feel better. I'll go make you some bread." She heads downstairs to the kitchen. Barrel's boys make me keep the door open while I have a shower, but that doesn't seem like such a big deal considering everything else. As I get dressed, I seriously consider jumping out the window, but I figure Barrel's boys would grab hold of me before I'd even get my head out. I don't want to know what the punishment would be for trying to get away. And besides, if I ran away, my debt wouldn't be paid off and they'd go after Dillon. I couldn't live with myself if something happened to him because of me. I try not to think about him, how furious and powerless and upset he must feel, being apart from me, knowing what I'm doing for him, for us.

# Chapter Seventeen

Two weeks pass. Where is Dillon? Barrel won't answer my questions. Kitty says she doesn't know, but I don't know if I should believe her or not. I've been trapped in Barrel's house the entire time. I haven't set foot outside even once. If this were the real world, he'd be arrested for kidnapping and unlawful confinement of a minor. The Barrel Boys took my clothes and my wallet with all of my ID. All I've got is one pair of underwear and a bra I wash out in the sink when I get a chance and this thin robe thing. When some sleazy lowlife pig who probably goes home to his wife and kids and pretends like he's a nice normal guy is not screwing me, I walk around wrapped up in a quilt. I've never been so cold in all my life.

I don't want to think about how many times I've been locked in that smelly room with creepy men and that enormous bed. I'm sure the debt has been paid by now. Kitty says Barrel's the one who decides when and if the debt's been erased.

"If?"

"If, Izzy." She hands me another slice of bread. "That's just how it goes around here. Come on, you must realize that by now."

I want to go home. Not to Dillon's place. Back to my house. I want Rob the Slob to drive drunk straight off a cliff and die. I want Mom to hurt herself at work so she'll never leave me alone again. I want Big Bad Barrel to eat some bad shellfish and die a slow, painful death. I'd watch. I swear I would. I'd stand right over him and laugh and spit on him and kick him. I would. I'd kick a dying man. That's how far I've sunk, never mind the business in the room with that enormous bed and the men with their serious body stink.

One day the Barrel Boy watching me falls asleep on the couch. They took my cell phone, so I sneak to the phone in the kitchen and call Margaret's house. Her mother answers.

"I heard you've quit school, Izzy," she says in her stick-up-her-butt way.

"Yeah, but I'm going back though."

"Oh?" I can hear her lick her lips. "And what do you think Mrs. Singh will make of that?"

"Just get me Margaret, okay?" The Barrel Boy is stirring. "I'm in a hurry."

"Don't take that tone with me, young lady."

"Get me Margaret!" I hiss. "It's an emergency!"

"I seem to recall that Margaret has stepped out just now, with Amanda."

"You're a stupid, fat cow, Mrs. Pritchard!"

"And you are a waste of my Margaret's time." She hangs up.

"Bitch!" I yell at the dial tone. That wakes the Barrel Boy. He gives me a clumsy whack that ends up in a couple of black eyes, but it's worth it, saying that to her. She's hated me since third grade.

I think the black eyes might get me out of work for a couple of days, but apparently it's no big deal to have black eyes in the game. That's what Kitty and the other girls call it. The game. What kind of game is it if you're always the loser?

I know the other girls' names now. Cherise and Lena. But just because I know their names doesn't mean I like them any better. They're snobs. They talk quietly in some kind of language they made up, kind of like pig Latin, only not quite, because then I'd understand them. They float around like ghosts, drifting upstairs in the morning and downstairs at night. They look hollow and mean and older than Kitty when she's in her grandmotherly mood. Cherise and Lena can come and go as they please. No one's looking for them. No one's waiting for them. They have nowhere to go. Who knows, maybe they like living like this.

One morning when they come in, Lena's arms are covered in bruises. Her top is ripped, and her lip is split and bloody. She lets Kitty fix her up. Cherise is too shaky to do it. I don't know if it's fright or if she's coming off coke or something. Those two like their coke, that's for sure. I'm wrapped in my quilt, a mug of hot apple juice warming my hands.

"Why don't you just leave?" I ask.

Lena winces, either from the question or from the antiseptic stuff Kitty's dabbing on her lip. I ask the question again. She doesn't answer.

"I mean, I can't leave." I glance through to the living room where my current Barrel Boy is watching a hockey game. "Mullet Man in there would chase me down and kill me. But you two could."

"Don't screw things up for us!" Cherise stands up suddenly. "You don't understand how things work around here!"

That's the most she's said to me in plain English, ever. Cherise helps Lena upstairs. Kitty frowns at me as she puts the first-aid kit away. She leaves the room and doesn't talk to me for the rest of the day.

# Chapter Eighteen

Dillon is back. Actually, he never went away. Kitty tells me this after she overhears a phone call between Dillon and Barrel.

"Just in case you ever thought he was your boyfriend," she says. She's been in a bitchy mood all day, probably her period.

"You don't mean that," I say.

"How else do you think Barrel gets his girls?" Her bread comes out hard as a rock. That makes her even more pissed off. "It was the same with me. The attention, the shopping, the whole works."

"It's different with Dillon. He'll come get me when the debt's paid off."

"It was with Dillon." Kitty chucks the bread into the garbage and slams the lid. Barrel hollers at us to shut up. There's a big hockey game on. He's got all his boys over to watch. A stack of pizzas came, but we're not allowed any.

"What do you mean?"

"It's all part of the game, Izzy." Kitty sits down. Her voice is a little shaky, like she's telling me all this against her will. "Me and Dillon. It was the same with me. I lived in that apartment for three months too."

"You're lying."

"Let me guess. For your three-month anniversary he took you to Casa Italiano and then to that motel up on Kingsway."

Someone scores a goal. Barrel and his boys cheer. I'm so angry I throw my mug at the window above the sink. The window and the mug shatter. Just as I'm reaching for something else to throw, Barrel and a couple of his boys storm in. The boys haul me up and shove my face at the jagged glass.

"You want to get sliced open, huh?" Barrel picks up a shard of glass and presses it to the skin under my eye. The first punch knocks me out.

When I come to, I can't open my eyes. At first I think he cut them, but I feel with my fingertips. No slices. But so swollen. I'm naked. My ribs are tender all over and it hurts to breathe.

My neck is stiff. My lip is fat. I'm in the basement; I can tell by the footsteps overhead and the hum of the furnace. I've only been down here once before. Barrel made me and the other girls watch his boys beat up the guy with the goatee. Something about money. He made us watch so that we'd stay afraid.

I am afraid.

## Chapter Nineteen

I don't know how long it was before I could open my eyes. When I could, it was dark. Upstairs there were voices, the muffled laugh track from some cheesy TV show, footsteps crossing from kitchen to living room, someone running up the stairs, then down again. I watched the road outside. There was a lot of traffic. I figured it must be about suppertime, everybody heading home to their normal lives, from normal jobs in offices and factories and warehouses. It was a busy, dirty, wide road. Not many people walked by that route. It's a mostly industrial part of town. I saw a few guys with lunch kits and hardhats. I waved and waved, but they never looked over, and they couldn't see me anyway. The basement was dark. Someone had taken away all the lightbulbs.

The smells of Kitty's famous chili and fresh-baked buns wafted under the door. Later, the stereo went on, there was dancing and partying, something major tipped over, maybe a shelf, or a person. After the longest time, people left; it grew silent upstairs and quiet outside. Time to go.

I found a nail and a brick and a bunch of dirty rags. I tapped the glass until it cracked and then carefully broke away each piece, catching them in the rags so they wouldn't fall to the floor and smash, waking them up upstairs.

I looked around for something to wear. There was nothing but oily rags and a great big moldy blue tarp. I shoved it through the window ahead of me. It would be better than being naked. I climbed out onto the cold, wet grass, my thigh getting sliced on a piece of glass I missed. It bled really bad, but there was nothing I could do about it. I was going to drape the tarp around me right there, but it made too much noise. I hobbled around to the front of the house, dragging the tarp behind me.

A voice broke the silence. "Psst! Over here!"

It was Cherise, smoking a cigarette on the porch. She threw me a sweater and a pair of pants. "We've been taking turns, waiting for you. Your phone rang. It was your mom. She's looking for you."

At first I thought she was speaking to me in her and Lena's secret language.

"My mom?" I said as I painfully shifted from one freezing bare foot to the other, struggling to get the pants on.

Cherise came down the steps to help me and saw all the blood.

"Wait here, I'll go get a bandage."

As she opened the front door, a light went on upstairs.

"You'd better go!"

I lifted my arms to put on the sweater, but the pain was so bad I couldn't do it.

"Just go!" Cherise shoved me into the street. "Run!"

But I couldn't. I hobbled away as fast as I could and ducked into a doorway. I waited for Cherise to follow me. She didn't. I saw Barrel drag her back inside, and then all the lights in the house went on.

I limped barefoot to the hospital, clutching the sweater to my naked chest.

The night nurse lept up when I dragged myself in.

"Oh, honey." She put her arms around me. "Let me help you."

I told the police Barrel's address, but when they went by an hour after I left, the house was empty, not even an empty beer can left behind.

Rob the Slob was gone too. Word got to Mom through one of the logger's wives that he was screwing around on her the whole time. That's why she came home early and was looking for me. Now she was all apologies, all the time.

"I'm sorry I didn't believe you."

"I'm sorry I went away."

"I'm sorry for what happened to you."

"I'm sorry about Rob."

I didn't go back to school, even though Mrs. Singh said I was welcome and Mom thought it would be best if things just got back to normal as soon as possible. I tried to explain to her that I didn't know what normal meant anymore, but she doesn't get it. She thinks normal is about things: school, friends, clothes, food, home.

I might go back to school in the fall. A different school, though. I might miss Margaret, a lot, but I can't be her friend right now. And she can't be mine, even if she does want to be. She came to see me in the hospital. She brought me flowers and a teddy bear and a box of chocolates and a stack of magazines. It's weird that people bring the same stupidly comforting things whether you're hospitalized after being beaten and consistently raped for weeks or if you're just having day surgery.

"My mom doesn't know," she said.

"That you're here? Or what I went through?"

"Either."

"Go away, Margaret."

"Please, Izzy? I'm sorry."

"You and everybody else."

"I told Amanda I'd pick you over her any day. I told her you were my best friend, not her."

It's when she said that that I knew. What a little-girl thing to say, how grade four, how playground, how tea set and dolls.

"That's right. Were. I'm not your best friend anymore."

"But you are!"

"No I'm not. Go away, okay? Just go away."

"But we've been best friends since third grade!"

"Well, this isn't third grade anymore."

She left in tears. I could hear her sniffling out in the hall, waiting for me to call her back. I flipped through one of the magazines, trying to disappear into the latest Hollywood gossip. When she finally left, I dumped everything she brought into the garbage. Later that day, though, when the cleaning staff came to take away the garbage, I took it all back and tucked the teddy bear under the blankets with me when the hospital lights dimmed for the night.

# Chapter Twenty

Mom and I put our stuff into storage, and I flew up north with her, to work as a kitchen apprentice at the logging camp. First a big plane, then a long drive to the ocean, then up in the shuddering floatplane off the water. I saw a moose ambling through an alpine field and a black bear just before we flew over the log sort. The plane landed with a little bounce on the waves and we taxied up to the dock. I climbed out, my breath puffing into the crisp cold morning. The smell of cedar, the calm lapping of the water in the sheltered harbor, the mist climbing the mountains, an eagle circling overhead, a heron taking off from the log boom, its wide blue wings lifting it up to the clouds. For the first time in months I felt normal.

I dumped my bags on my bunk and ran along the boardwalk to the dining hall. As soon as I stepped into that wood-smoke kitchen, I just wanted to crawl into the metal cupboards and sing to hear my own voice echo. So I did. That's where Mom found me when she finally caught up. She peered in at me singing to myself and laughed. She actually laughed. When I crawled out, I found a big ceramic bowl and the bucket of flour and got busy teaching her how to make bread.